First U.S. Edition   1 2 3 4 5 6 7 8 9 10

Library of Congress Cataloging in Publication Data
Ormerod, Jan. Come back, puppies / Jan Ormerod.
p.   cm.   Summary: Readers can find the missing puppies by turning
colorful acetate pages.   ISBN 0-688-09135-0   1. Toy and movable
books—Specimens.   [1. Dogs—Fiction.   2. Toy and movable books.]
I. Title. PZ7.0634Cp 1992 [E]—dc20 91-30424 CIP AC

COME BACK, PUPPIES

Jan Ormerod

LOTHROP, LEE & SHEPARD BOOKS
NEW YORK

Where are all my puppies?
Come back, puppies.

Where is the cream puppy?
Come back, puppy.

Where are the
golden puppies?
Come back, puppies.

Dinner's nearly ready.
But where are all
the other puppies?
Come back, puppies.

Where are all
the brown puppies?
Come back, puppies.

Where are all
the brown puppies?
Come back, puppies.

Dinner's nearly ready.
But where are all
the other puppies?
Come back, puppies.

Where are all
the black puppies?
Come back, puppies.

The little spotted puppy
was here all the time.
Can you count the puppies?